PTS-2.0
RLU.7

CHLOE *by* DESIGN

RUNWAY
Rundown

BY MARGARET GUREVICH

ILLUSTRATIONS & PHOTOS BY BROOKE HAGEL

STONE ARCH BOOKS
a capstone imprint

Chloe by Design is published by Stone Arch Books
A Capstone Imprint
1710 Roe Crest Drive
North Mankato, MN 56003
www.capstonepub.com

Text and illustrations © 2016 Stone Arch Books

Library of Congress Cataloging-in-Publication Data
Gurevich, Margaret, author.
Runway rundown / by Margaret Gurevich; illustrations by Brooke Hagel.
pages cm. -- (Chloe by design)

Summary: As Fashion Week approaches, Chloe's internship expands to
take in a third department, public relations, which is exciting and fun —
but when she is pulled in as a guest judge on this year's *Teen Design Diva*
show, her frantic schedule interferes with her relationship with Jake, her
boyfriend.

ISBN 978-1-4965-0506-4 (hardcover) -- ISBN 978-1-4965-2312-9 (ebook pdf)

1. Fashion design--Study and teaching (Internship)--Juvenile fiction.
2. Fashion designers--Juvenile fiction. 3. Internship programs--Juvenile
fiction. 4. Television game shows--Juvenile fiction. 5. Dating (Social
customs)--Juvenile fiction. 6. Friendship--Juvenile fiction. 7. New York
(N.Y.)--Juvenile fiction. [1. Fashion design--Fiction. 2. Internship programs-
-Fiction. 3. Reality television programs--Fiction. 4. Dating (Social customs)-
-Fiction. 5. Friendship--Fiction. 6. New York (N.Y.)--Fiction.] I. Hagel,
Brooke, illustrator. II. Title. III. Series: Gurevich, Margaret. Chloe by design.
PZ7.G98146Ru 2016
813.6--dc23 [Fic]

2014043695

Designer: Alison Thiele
Editor: Alison Deering

Artistic Elements: Shutterstock

Printed in the United States of America in Stevens Point, Wisconsin.
042015   008824WZF15

Measure twice, cut once
or you won't make the cut.

Dear Diary,

I can't believe I'm already done with the first month of my Stefan Meyers internship! I only have a month left until it's time to head back to my real life in California — more importantly, though, only three weeks until Fashion Week!

Living in New York has been amazing. Not only do I get to explore the city, I also get to stay in the dorms at FIT, my dream school! For the most part, my roommates are great. Well . . . at least two of them. Avery and Bailey are sweet and fun, but Madison has had it out for me since day one. She acts like I don't belong here because I won my internship on *Teen Design Diva*.

But back to the important stuff — Fashion Week. It has all my roommates on edge. Bailey keeps telling me, "Until everything comes together, it'll be total chaos — like a tornado, monsoon, and hailstorm combined." I'm trying to stay calm, but Bailey has interned before and knows the business better than I do, so her doomsday thinking is freaking me out just a little.

I have enough to worry about without the added stress. I've been rotating departments every two weeks at work. So far, I've been in knits with Laura and dresses with Taylor. Tomorrow I start in public relations with Michael — for part of the week, anyway. Laura needs me too, so I'll work with her on Thursday and Friday and spend the other three days with Michael. Supposedly PR is super glam and can include working with the *Vogue* crew and dealing with the media. It's thrilling, but it's also a lot of pressure. I just hope I don't mess something up.

I mentioned all this to Alex, my best friend back home, and she told me to go with the flow. And when I talked to Jake — my sort of friend, sort of crush — he said the same thing. Easy for them to say! But both of them have been my cheerleaders since this whole thing started, so maybe they're right. Maybe I just need to relax and go with the flow . . . but for now, I'd better get some sleep. Big day tomorrow!

Xoxo — Chloe

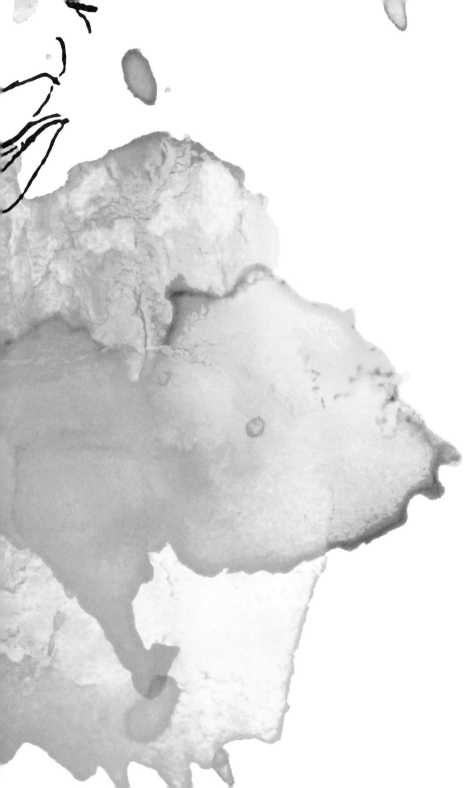

On Monday morning, I stand in front of the mirror and give myself the once-over. Since Stefan said PR is all about glitz and glam, I'm using today as an opportunity to wear one of the outfits I created during the *Teen Design Diva* competition — my final winning design. I slip into the monochromatic tailored shift dress, complete with metallic accents, and do a spin in front of the mirror.

Once I get to the Stefan Meyers headquarters, though, my nerves get the best of me. Every time I start to feel comfortable in a department, it's time to embark on a new challenge. I wish Laura, Taylor, or even Stefan were here to make today's transition easier.

I take a deep breath and open the door to the lobby. *You got this, Chloe*, I tell myself.

DESIGN DIVA
FINAL
Design

REMOVABLE
COLLAR FOR
EVENTS

Night Look

ACCESSORIZE WITH
GOLD EARRINGS
& SHOES

"Good morning, Miss Montgomery," says Ken, the security guard.

"Good morning," I say, showing my ID card.

Ken's familiar face usually puts me at ease, but today my stomach is participating in a full-on gymnastics competition. I pull out my phone and check the e-mail Stefan sent me with instructions, then head to the elevator and press the button for the twelfth floor.

When the elevator stops at my floor and the doors slide open, I'm shocked at what I see. Laura's and Taylor's departments had inspiration boards, mannequins, and fabric in every corner, but they were relatively quiet. People were either cutting material, sketching, or measuring garments. This floor is more organized, but it's *loud*. Everyone is either on the phone or typing something on the computer or shouting to someone else.

I glance at the e-mail, but it doesn't say where I can find Michael. "Excuse me," I say to a woman in one of the cubicles, "is Michael here?"

"One sec," she says. At almost the same moment, someone with a British accent says, "I'm right here."

I spin around. The man facing me has black hair that's tied back neatly in a ponytail. His warm amber eyes twinkle when he smiles. "I'm Michael Travers," he says, extending his hand.

"Chloe Montgomery," I reply, shaking his hand.

"Nice to meet you, Chloe," Michael says. "I've heard good things about you so far. I'm looking forward to working with you."

"Me too," I say. His accent sounds so proper, I feel like I should be watching my grammar or something.

"Splendid." Michael claps his hands. "What do you know about PR?"

I feel dumb already. All I know is that Stefan said something about glamour and celebs. "Um . . . not much," I admit.

Michael grins as though that's the greatest news he's ever heard. "That's wonderful! Truly wonderful!" he says. "The worst is an overly confident college kid who thinks he knows more than I do. You, my dear, are a blank slate."

"Um, thanks?" I'm glad he finds my ignorance useful.

"Don't be embarrassed," Michael says. "I'm here to teach you." He leads me into his office and motions for me to sit in one of the empty chairs. "Sorry for the mess."

Michael's definition of mess is very different from mine. All the papers on his desk are neatly organized into piles, his trash is nowhere near overflowing, and his coffee cup is resting on a coaster. There are dressers lining the office from door to window, each one chock full of Stefan's dresses, pantsuits, and denim items. I'd take a mess like this any day. If Laura had an office that looked like this, she'd be thrilled.

"It's amazing," I say.

"I suppose, but all this stuff is driving me batty." He sighs. "Thank goodness you'll be helping me with some of it today."

I'm confused. "Did you want me to organize all this for you?"

Michael looks surprised. "Goodness, no! This is as organized as it's going to get. You'll be assisting with clothing transport. It's not a very teachable moment, I'm afraid, but it's a necessity."

"Transport to where?" I ask.

"We've secured a placement in *Vogue* for some of Stefan's new pieces," Michael explains, "but I just received an e-mail saying they need the designs today instead of next week."

"Oh, wow," I say.

"I know — tight deadline," Michael agrees. "We'll start by going through these racks. I'll pick out five pieces that will show well, and then I'll be sending you to Laura and Taylor to pick up additional garments. Normally, we package and send things over. But because of the tight deadline and our proximity to *Vogue*, we'll get them ready, and you'll carry them yourself. Clear?"

I nod. The thought of my arms loaded with heavy clothes as I walk the streets of New York City is slightly overwhelming. I become extra conscious of today's outfit. It's perfect for dinner at an upscale club. Trudging through the heat, saddled like a mule? Not so much.

Just then Michael notices my heels. "Tell me you have other shoes," he says, sounding concerned.

I shake my head. "Not with me."

"Then let's hope those are more comfortable than they look."

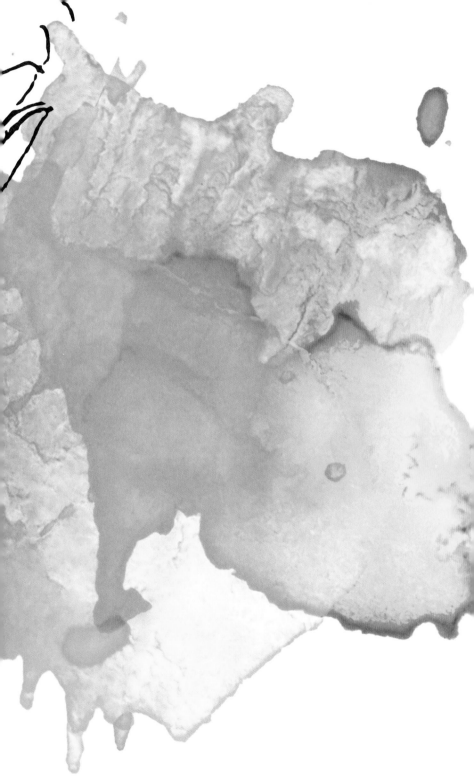

An hour later, my arms are loaded with two pairs of patterned jeans, a denim blouse with a velvet collar, and two dresses with embroidered pockets — pockets I designed! Michael had everything packaged in garment bags for easier transport, but they still weigh a ton.

My next stop is Laura's office. When I arrive, she has several garment bags all ready to go.

"Nothing like tight deadlines," Laura says. She unzips each bag to show me the pieces I'll be carrying, including an art deco-patterned sweater dress and a pantsuit. "It was really difficult to choose which designs to showcase since Stefan wanted to incorporate so many into Fashion Week. But we managed to part with a few he won't be showing."

I study the garments again. I don't see anything I've worked on, but maybe that means some of the items I helped with are being saved for Fashion Week.

VOGUE PHOTOSHOOT *Designs*

Neutral Color Palette

PINSTRIPE SUIT

ART DECO SWEATER DRESS

SLIM-FIT PANTS

LONG LACE HEM

"Do you think I'll get to work with the stylists at *Vogue*? Will Anna Wintour be around?" I blurt out.

Laura's sympathetic face makes me feel silly. "Stefan talked up PR too much," she says. "There will be some cool stuff too, don't worry. But fashion isn't all glamorous. Remember when you sorted the closet on your first day here? It got better, right?"

I laugh. "Right. See you Thursday!"

"Counting down the days!" Laura calls as I leave her office.

Taylor is my last stop. As usual, her hair is pulled back in a bun, and she looks cool, calm, and collected. Her desk is covered with pieces of gold jewelry cascading down like a waterfall. I wonder if that's part of her Fashion Week collaboration with Liesel McKay, my former *Design Diva* mentor and Jake's mom.

"I have everything ready for you," Taylor says, not getting up from behind her desk.

I spot a bag with five hangers sticking out the top sitting on a nearby chair and shift the garments Michael and Laura gave me to my other arm. The weight is bearing down on me, and my toes are starting to look like sausages.

Very attractive, Chloe, I think.

I open the bags to take a peek, and my breath catches when I see the beautiful silk dresses I worked on. The last time I saw them they were only prototypes; now they're full-fledged garments. The sparkly beading on the bodice of one of the pieces glistens in the light.

"Thanks," I say, grabbing the bag.

Taylor looks up from her work, then glances down at my feet. "You have no other shoes with you?"

I groan. I hope my cute silver heels don't become a death sentence for my feet. "Unfortunately not," I say.

Taylor raises an eyebrow. "Bring flip-flops from now on." With that, she hunches back over her jewelry.

* * *

The sun beats down on me as I make the trek to *Vogue*. I shift the bags from arm to arm and try to ignore the blisters on my toes and the sweat seeping down my dress. My phone buzzes, but I'm too loaded down to reach it.

I finally walk through the revolving doors and am hit with a blast of cool air. The security guard checks me in and doesn't even blink at my disheveled appearance. As I step into the elevator and ride it up to the eighth floor, a part of me still hopes to run into someone important. I imagine getting a tour of the office, seeing famous models up close, watching a photo shoot.

But my hopes are dashed as soon as the doors open. A girl not much older than me is waiting. She smiles sympathetically. "I hope you didn't have a far walk. Life of an intern, huh?"

"How did you —" I start to ask, but the answer is pretty obvious. Who else would be lugging stuff across city streets?

The girl puts her arms out, and I hand over the bags. "They're heavy!" she exclaims. Just then her phone rings, prompting an eye-roll. "My boss has texted me three times already. I don't know what she thinks I'm doing!"

Without another word, the girl waves goodbye and rushes off. So much for a *Vogue* tour.

The walk back to Stefan Meyers is much easier without the bags, but my toes are bleeding from my high heels, so I buy a pair of cheap flip-flops from a vendor and put them on.

My phone buzzes again, and I pull it out. I have two texts, both from Jake. The first is a photo of a soft pretzel, my favorite snack. The other says, "Can you tear yourself away from your glamorous life to have lunch with a commoner?"

I can't help but smile. If only he could see me now. My flip-flops and throbbing shoulders are hardly the epitome of glam. I miss Jake, but the thought of putting on real shoes and walking anywhere makes my feet hurt even more.

"Dinner?" I text back.

"Class :-(" he replies.

I sigh and type, "Rain check" as I rush back to the office to rest my feet.

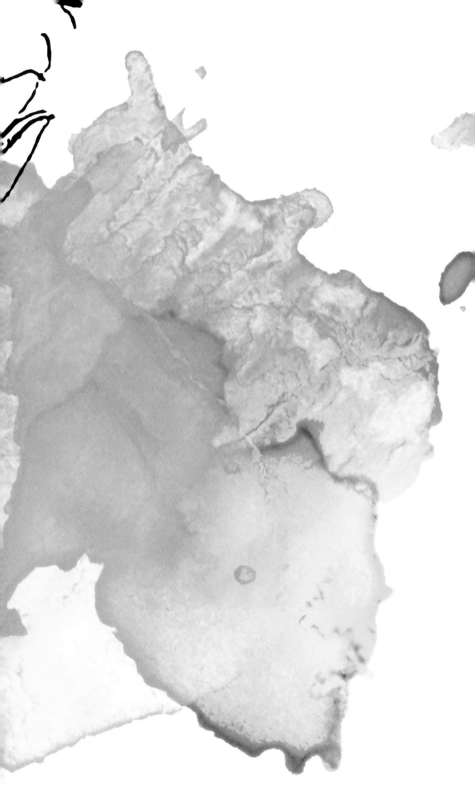

The next morning, my feet feel slightly more normal, and my bag is prepped with flip-flops. When I arrive at work, there's a cup of coffee already waiting at my desk.

"Is this yours?" I ask Michael, lifting the cup.

He chuckles. "No, my dear. That's for you. A thank-you for your hard work."

"This must be the glam part Stefan promised," I say.

Michael laughs. "You're funny."

I smile as I take a grateful sip. If today is anything like yesterday, I'll definitely need the caffeine.

"Today," says Michael, pulling a swivel chair up beside my desk, "you're going to learn about the press release and e-mail blast. Both are intended to get the word out about our brand. We want Stefan Meyers's styles to be seen everywhere — news media, magazines, newspapers, fashion networks."

I find myself leaning forward in my chair, caught up in his enthusiasm.

"The e-mail blast focuses on snappy facts and catchy headlines that will quickly grab readers' attention," he continues. "Journalists get hundreds of blasts a day, so ours needs to stand out. Even though the blast is more common, we do old-fashioned press releases too."

"Why?" I ask. I like the idea of short and snappy. It doesn't seem to make sense to bore people with something longer.

Michael beams as if my question is brilliant. "I love that you're thinking!" he says. "The longer press releases are perfect for new product launches. Say Stefan wanted to expand his brand into something he's never done before, like baby clothes."

I laugh. "I cannot imagine Stefan Meyers doing baby clothes."

"Exactly," says Michael. "Something so different would require more info. If an editor just saw 'Stefan Meyers Dresses Babies' as a headline, he'd think it was a joke. We also supply press releases to media outlets that prefer additional information when writing their stories. Some like the extra facts to bulk up their articles."

Michael goes into his office and comes back with a coffee for himself. "We'll start with the press release and then pull facts from that for the e-mail blast. What do you know about writing?"

"Like essays?" I say. I hate essays.

Michael laughs. "Hardly. Even with the longer press release, our goal is to create something that can wow in under a page."

I frown. Writing and I don't exactly mix.

"Don't worry," says Michael, reading my face. "We'll work on them together. First thing you have to do is forget what they taught you in school about writing."

I like this task! "Done!" I say with a laugh.

Michael grins. "Well, maybe not everything. You definitely want whatever we send to be free of grammatical errors. But don't worry about fancy vocabulary or a lot of description. The details have to grab the reader's attention quickly. Snappy titles are key too."

He shows me a template that says to focus on the five *w*'s — Who, What, When, Where, Why — and the *h* — How. Our English teacher actually said the same thing, but I keep that to myself. "We'll focus this first piece on Stefan's spring line," he says.

"The *who* is easy," I say. "Stefan Meyers."

Michael writes that down. "Good."

"The *what* can be so many things, though," I say. "Denims, spring line?"

Michael taps his pencil on his chin thoughtfully. "Those are all good, but we want to wow. So what's the special line Stefan is working on?"

"Art deco!" I exclaim a little too loudly.

"Exactly," says Michael, writing that in the *what* column.

When and *where* are easy, and Michael fills in Fashion Week and Lincoln Center respectively. "What about the *why*?" he asks.

I brainstorm out loud. "To bring back old-world glitz, the excitement of the Roaring Twenties, and to modernize old-style glamour?"

Michael writes down all my suggestions. "I like the last one a lot," he said. "We'll work on expanding that. That just leaves us with the *how*."

I check the notes on my laptop about the *w*'s and something clicks. "Does that mean the specifics of the fashion show? Explaining the looks and theme?"

Michael nods. "You got it."

I'm feeling more relaxed than when we started. Having this broken down with Michael makes it seem way less daunting.

"So what we have here is a great start, but it's just the bare bones," he says. "For the release, all these things have to be expanded. I've heard from Laura, Taylor, and Stefan that you have a great eye for fashion and really understand the new art deco line."

I blush. "Thanks."

"I want you to use that knowledge to expand on the *what*. Describe the fabric and cut of the pieces. Elaborate on the design. If you were trying to sell Taylor's dresses to someone, what would you focus on?"

This is more my speed. I take out my sketchpad and flip through the designs I did for Laura and Taylor.

"I'll let you get started on this on your own and come check up on you in an hour. Deal?" says Michael, handing me the notes he wrote. Now I can reference his and mine.

"Deal," I agree, eager to get into my design comfort zone.

Michael heads out, and I flip through my sketches, looking at my fabric descriptions. Taylor's dresses are silk and satin and feature unique details like hand-sewn beading. I also know the jewelry is handmade. I close my eyes, remembering the gold jewelry I saw in Taylor's office yesterday. It reminded me of cascading water. I scribble that in my notes and think about how to add attention-grabbing details.

When Michael stops by an hour later, I have a few solid paragraphs I'm proud of.

"Let's take a look," he says, pulling his chair closer. He reads my descriptions and smiles. "I like what you've done here. You really help the reader visualize the garments. It's clear you get Stefan's designs." He scrolls down. "Nice touch describing the jewelry piece as 'avant-garde.' And I like that you compared it to a waterfall. That's a nice image. I'll think about how to fine-tune this part where you describe the art deco style ranging from 'black-tie glamorous to daily chic,' but I like where you're going with it. Excellent for a first attempt."

"Thank you," I say. But there are still four more *w*'s and an *h* to tackle. "I didn't really know what to do with the heading and stuff."

"You have the hard part down," Michael says. "You know the designs and fabrics. The rest is easy." He goes into his office and returns with a binder. "I'm going to go over these old press releases with you, but I'll also let you take the binder home. I've also catalogued some of my favorite headlines from magazines and the industry. You can always learn from others. I'd like you to come up with at least three headline options for the press release. We'll use the same ones in the e-mail blasts, so we have to make sure they're eye-catching and sharp."

I flip through the binder. "I like this one about a basketball player's new shoe line," I say. "'Damian's Heart and Sole Endeavor.'"

"It's silly," says Michael. "But it gets your attention."

I look through more examples and stop at a reality celeb's clothing venture. "'Reassessing Frumpy Chic'?"

Michael laughs. "That design tanked, but the headline got a lot of people talking. Frumpy and chic don't go together at all, and people were dying to see the connection."

I think I'm starting to get the idea. The headlines can be funny or shocking or sophisticated, as long as they leave the reader wanting more. "This is a good one too," I say, "'Designers Revive Polka-Dot Sophistication.' I've never thought polka-dots needed a revival or that they were sophisticated!"

"That's what I liked about it too," Michael agrees. "It was unexpected. Keep that in mind while you brainstorm. I look forward to seeing what you come up with."

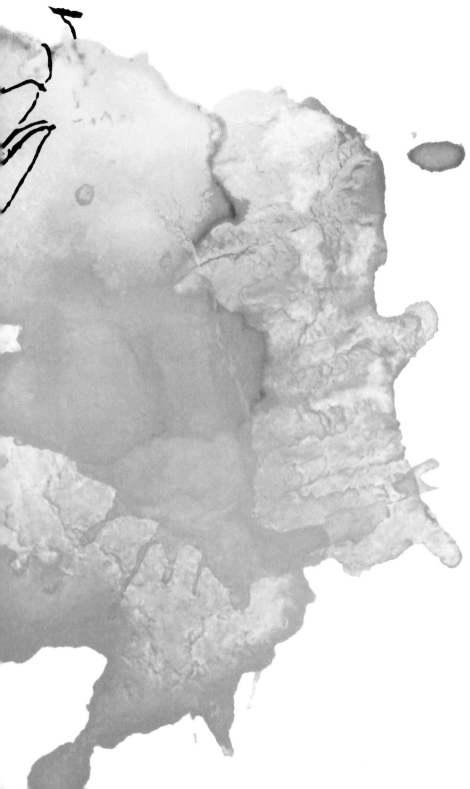

Wednesday morning, I have six headlines ready to go. I know, I know — overachiever much? But I want Michael to know I took this seriously. After all, writing isn't exactly my strong suit. I even took a stab at expanding the *who* portion of the release based on the information about Stefan in the binder.

Unfortunately, when I get to work, Michael seems too busy to be impressed. He breezes past me, sending papers flying off my desk. "It's going to be a crazy day," he says. Just then he notices the envelope I'm holding labeled PRESS RELEASE. "Oh, good, you finished! I can't wait to see it."

Michael takes the envelope and motions for me to follow him to his office. "You expanded the bio information!" he says, reading it over. "That's fabulous. And it looks like you managed to work in all the main points in the binder, including Stefan's award-winning fall line and his charity involvement. There are a few new updates to Stefan's career I didn't have in the binder, but I'll add them myself. Well done."

"Thanks," I reply, blushing a little.

Michael moves on to my headlines. The first one, "Stefan Unveils Art Deco Magic" was one of my first tries.

"It's good you mention the art deco upfront," Michael says, "but it doesn't say much. What does 'magic' *mean*, you know?"

I nod. That wasn't my favorite either, but I was hoping Michael would disagree. I guess they can't all be winners, though.

Michael keeps going down the list. "This is better," he says. "'Stefan Meyers Brings Back Roaring Twenties.' But I'm interested in *what* he's doing to bring that back. That's my hook."

That headline was one of my favorites, and I'm a little disappointed Michael isn't totally wowed by it.

"This one," says Michael, pointing to my last headline, "focuses on what Stefan wants to get out about his line. 'Stefan Meyers — Regal, Elegant, Art Deco Line.' It hints at what Stefan's line will be about without hitting readers over the head."

Michael rubs his chin. "Let's combine my two favorites. How about 'Stefan Meyers Brings Back Roaring Twenties with Elegant Art Deco Line.'"

"I love that!" I say, impressed at how quickly he was able to pull out the best parts of both headlines and turn them into something great.

"I'm going to finish fine-tuning the release," Michael tells me. "You, however, were promised glam. Today, you'll get to work on a project that should meet those expectations." He wheels a cart full of fashion and tabloid magazines over to me. "Are you familiar with these?"

Familiar? Alex and I have spent entire weekends flipping through magazines like these and dissecting each page. "I live for them!" I reply.

Michael laughs. "Breathe in as many as you can. That's today's task."

I stare at him, feeling confused. "You want me to read fashion mags all day?" I ask. That sounds too good to be true.

"Not just read," Michael says. "Scrutinize. I want you to peruse the pages and make notes of which celebs are wearing Stefan Meyers. Then, you'll scour celebrity Instagram accounts for the same thing. When you're done, we'll compile a list and use the information for publicity material. We'll know which celebrities to approach in the future about wearing our designs. Any questions?"

"Nope," I say quickly. Best. Assignment. Ever.

* * *

I spend the rest of the day taking notes, even eating lunch at my desk, but it's totally worth it. I make sure my information includes the celeb's name, the links or pages to the designs, and a description of the outfit worn.

I spot an image of Lola Corrigan, my favorite actress, in a tan suede jacket and black skirt and remember dragging Alex to the television so we could get a closer look when they dissected it on *Fashion Police*.

I find a shot of Hunter Bancroft, one of the *Design Diva* judges, wearing a pair of Stefan Meyers corduroy slacks. Each leg panel is done in a different color. It's just the type of out-of-the-box style Hunter enjoys, and he pulls it off.

I send a photo to Jake, knowing he'd never wear the design. His style is much simpler and more masculine. His mom might be a famous designer, but Jake is a jeans-and-T-shirt guy all the way.

"Your new pants?" I type.

I get a response right away. "If Hunter can wear them, so can I! :-)" Jake writes back.

"Hope to see that soon!" I reply. I really miss Jake. I thought I'd see him way more once I was in New York, but I've hardly seen him at all. I've just been so busy with my internship. And with Fashion Week fast approaching, I don't see that changing anytime soon.

"Me too! Miss you!" Jake texts.

I smile. It's good to know he feels the same way.

I flip through more accounts and stumble upon Cassie McRay, Alex's favorite basketball player, wearing a Stefan Meyers tankini. I had no idea Stefan had a bathing suit line! I love the bright colors on the suit and send a link to Alex.

I go through dozens of accounts and more than fifty magazines. When it's time to go home, I'm exhausted, but I'm also inspired. I think about what I would do if I had my own line. Would I focus on everyday and eveningwear or be more versatile, like Stefan? I guess only time will tell.

TAN SUEDE
JACKET

FUNKY
ACCESSORIES

BLACK
PENCIL
SKIRT

TANKINI

GOLD
STILETTOS

RESEARCH
STEFAN MEYERS
Designs

DOODLES
& *Ideas*

ART
DECO
GLAM

EDGY
METALLICS

RUFFLES
& JEWEL
TONES

JACKETS
&
PANTS

FULL SKIRTS & FITTED BODICE

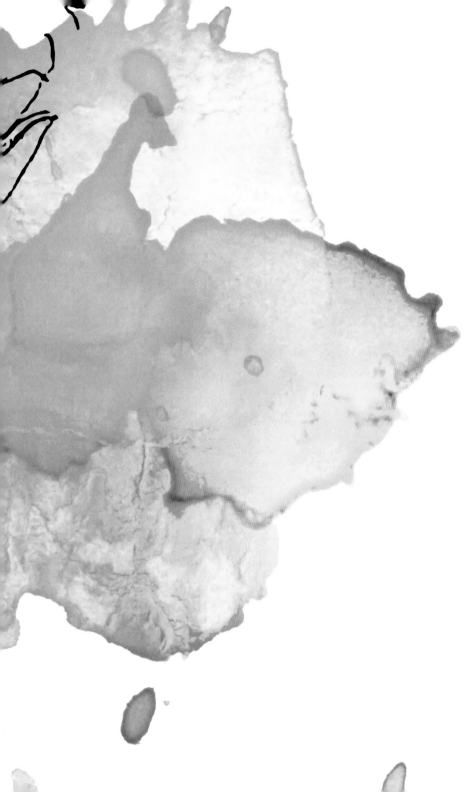

5

On Thursday, my first day back with Laura, I'm up bright and early. Sitting up in bed, I stick in my headphones, pick up my pencils and sketchpad, and start drawing.

I sketch wrap dresses with curved and plunging necklines in multiple colors. I add details to sleeves, hems, and collars like I've seen on some of Stefan's pieces. During *Design Diva*, I saw how tiny additions could really set a piece apart, and now, in the midst of the fashion industry, I'm noticing that even more.

Using a tan pencil, I color a pair of silky geometric-patterned shorts. I think about Stefan's art deco motif and shade in the shapes with a salmon pencil, then pair them with a solid-color blouse. A salmon-colored handbag with gold clasps completes the look.

IDEAS AND *Designs*

SOLID SILK TOP

PATTERNED SHORTS

HEELED BOOTIES

SALMON BAG

WRAP DRESSES

Suddenly someone taps my shoulder, and I'm so startled I almost fall off the bed. I pull out my headphones and turn and see Avery, one of my suitemates, standing there.

"Sorry, I didn't mean to scare you," she says. "Your door was open."

"That's okay." I look at the clock. "I should get going soon anyway. I don't want to be late."

"Where are you today?" Avery asks.

"With Laura," I reply. "I think she's finishing stuff for Fashion Week. I was in PR Monday, Tuesday, and Wednesday. How about you?"

"I'm in marketing and advertising now," Avery replies. "I really like it so far. I was watching you sketch, and you had this calm, happy look on your face. I'm not like that when I'm trying to design. It's so stressful! But with advertising, we have to do ad campaigns and think of slogans, and I love it. It just comes to me." She smiles.

"That's great," I say.

Avery looks relieved. "I know. I thought I messed up by choosing fashion as my major. It's a relief to see that there are other ways to work in this field. So much depends on how you present a piece to the world. I'm working on a campaign for 'chic sneaks' right now, and the goal is to show that the sneaker can be a workout shoe in one light, but dressy in another. We've gone through a few drafts of ad campaigns trying to make that balance obvious."

"My friend, Jake McKay, the one who came by the room before, is a marketing major too. Until he explained what he does, I never realized how important a campaign was, either! You really have to find the right buyer, huh?" I ask.

"Exactly," says Avery. "It's just such a relief to find my place!" She looks at her watch. "I'd better go, but thanks for chatting."

"See you soon!" I say, glad I could help. Avery is already in college and must have been scared when she didn't love every moment of her internship. We all have doubts, I realize.

I think again about how lucky I am to have this opportunity while I'm still in high school. I realize something else too. Not every part of an internship is a dream, but that's what makes it real.

* * *

"How's PR going?" Laura asks when I arrive at the office an hour later.

"It's cool!" I reply. "I love learning about the different departments. Yesterday, I got to look at magazines all day."

Laura's smile looks forced. Does she think I like working with Michael more than with her?

"Designing is still my passion," I reassure her. "I don't think all the glitz in the world will change that."

"Well, what I've seen so far has really impressed me. Let's put all that talent to good use." Laura winks at me and gets busy laying out prototypes.

There's a black blouse with white triangles. Another shirt is cotton with an art deco-inspired chevron pattern. Both items have smooth, mother-of-pearl buttons down the front.

"These are additions to Stefan's art deco line," says Laura. "He wants to add some menswear-inspired pieces for versatility. Notice the geometric patterns, which are key elements. I want you to study these prototypes. Then go on Stefan's website and take notes on his menswear as well. Pay special attention to the patterns, cuffs, and collars. Notice which he uses most frequently."

I nod. I can do that. I'm used to inspecting designs and taking note of common elements or what sets them apart.

"Once you've done that, I'd like you to take a stab at your own menswear-inspired sketches," says Laura.

I bite my lip. In all my years of designing, I've never created men's clothing. All my sketches were things I wanted to wear myself. "Um . . . I don't normally design men's stuff."

SHIRT PROTOTYPE Designs

- Pop of Color
- Menswear
- Spring Line

COLLAR & CUFFS

TRIANGLE PRINTED BLOUSE

GRAY SKINNY PANTS

CHEVRON PATTERN

YELLOW SKINNY PANTS

"That's okay — this is just menswear-inspired. Think about some masculine elements and how you could make them more wearable for women. We'll discuss them together when you're finished," says Laura. "You can do it."

Laura heads back to her office, and I pull up Stefan's site, still feeling a bit uncertain. I plow through page after page of menswear, making note of the slim fit that seems to be a constant through formal, sports, and office wear. I notice Stefan's signature buttoned barrel cuffs and variety of open collars.

Laura mentioned that Stefan wants these pieces to be part of the art deco collection, so I search online for images of men in the 1920s and 1930s. There are photos of men in braces — suspenders with buttons — and with pocket squares. I also notice a lot of hats — Panama hats, bowlers, fedoras — and pinstripes. Now I just have to translate those styles into something a modern woman would wear. Easy, right? Not.

My first few sketches, a mash-up of preppy and formalwear, find a home in the trash. In my head, the final product is stylish, but I can't seem to get the same result in my sketchpad. The next few drawings resemble something a kid would wear playing dress-up.

I try a different approach and sketch the items separately. Slim-fit shirts in a variety of patterns fill my pages. I add some wrap blouses to the mix for a more feminine silhouette, then add vintage-inspired and classic collars. Next, I play with the cuffs, making some barrel, others French. I add exaggerated cuffs to some of the wide-leg pants I've sketched as well.

Once I've nailed the shape, I move on to patterns, adding pinstripes to a sleeveless blouse. Another, I detail with converging silver lines. I experiment with only adding art deco elements to the pocket squares and braces, leaving the shirts solid.

Soon, my sketchpad is filled with a new section of menswear-inspired designs. I take them out to Laura's desk to show her what I've done, but she shakes her head, and my heart drops. I really thought I had nailed this assignment.

"Sorry," I say quietly. "I guess I missed the mark."

Laura looks surprised. "Not at all! I just didn't expect you to excel so quickly at this too."

What's that supposed to mean? I think. *Did she not want me to do well?*

The confusion must show on my face because Laura says, "That came out wrong. I can tell you're very talented, but when Stefan suggested you work on this, I was worried. I know you don't have much experience with men's clothing, and I was afraid you'd get discouraged.

You're a hard worker, Chloe, but you take a lot to heart. I didn't want you to get down on yourself."

I get what she means. My mom has had very similar advice for me in the past. "I know this internship is about learning, but I still want to be . . ." I search for the right word.

"Perfect?" Laura says with a laugh. "Honey, who is? If you keep measuring yourself by such high standards, you'll burn out before you've made a spark."

I sigh. "I know."

"But you did impress me," she continues. "It's clear you took your time with both the prototypes and the website. I like your variety of collars and patterns. And the silhouette of this wrap top is a great way to make menswear more accessible to women. The wrap really works well with the pinstripes — it helps soften the lines."

Laura flips through the sketches again. "I'd like to see these in more colors, and I want prototypes of the pinstripe blouse for the board. Nice work."

I head back to my desk, thinking about what Laura said about burning out. Striving for perfection is what got me here. How can wanting to succeed in everything be bad?

STRIPED PANTS

Neut~
Black
S~

GOLD ACCENTS

-PINSTRIPE
-Cuffs
-collars
-Tailored

WAIST ACCENTS

killer cuffs

high collar

Feminine Colors?

MENSWEAR
DEVELOPMENT
Sketches

MENSWEAR
FINAL
Design

BUCKET
HAT

WRAP
TOP

GOLD BEADED
PINSTRIPE

WIDE-LEG
PANTS

TUXEDO
STRIPE

I'm with Laura again on Friday, and the day goes smoothly. I'm starting to feel more comfortable with the menswear-inspired pieces. I especially like getting lost in the fine details of the cuffs and collars. I even find myself noticing the shirts men wear. From the sporty to the dressy, they all have a unique fit.

As the day draws to a close, I think about Jake. We haven't seen each other in two weeks, and texting just isn't the same. Hopefully, we'll get to hang out this weekend.

As if reading my mind, Laura says, "Michael would like you to see him. He has a weekend assignment for you."

I sigh. *Homework on the weekend? Really?* But I try not to be too upset. If this is what it takes to make it in the fashion world, there's no point in complaining.

Michael is waiting for me when I get to his office. "Do you know what market research is?" he asks.

"Uh, like researching the market?" I guess, going for the most obvious explanation. The truth is, I have no idea what this means.

Michael grins. "Exactly. Have it ready for me Monday!"

I panic. Is he serious?

Suddenly, Michael bursts out laughing. "Just teasing. Here's the deal — we're looking for you to see what's out there. Look at the items shoppers gravitate toward. Check out the trends, as well as what's on the clearance rack. Compare other designers' prices with ours. If something catches your eye, sketch it. Don't try to analyze why you're drawn to it, or you might miss something."

I perk up. This is unlike any homework assignment I've had before. "Do you want me to take notes on specific lines or designs?"

Michael shakes his head. "Nope. I don't want you to think too hard. I want to see what *you* think is important. You'd be surprised what we can learn this way."

"But I don't know this industry like you do," I say. "What if I miss something?"

"Your inexperience is precisely why you're perfect. You'll view items from a different perspective than a professional. A less-experienced eye might pick up on a detail or a trend that someone else would pass over," says Michael.

I've never thought of it that way, but it makes total sense. "Can I take pictures?" I ask. I imagine lurking behind displays and sneaking photos of different outfits.

"That would be helpful," Michael says, "but most stores no longer allow that because of security issues. Better to sketch instead."

My face falls. "I liked thinking of myself as a spy," I say sheepishly.

Michael's face grows serious. "You still are. We're counting on you to report back with valuable information. Here are your instructions and the stores to hit." He gives me a large manila envelope. "Agent Chloe Montgomery, will you accept your assignment?"

I hold back a smile. "I will."

* * *

"Going to rob a bank?" asks Madison when she sees my outfit Saturday morning.

I roll my eyes. Maybe I've taken this spy thing too far, but it's too fun not to! I'm dressed in a black romper and have a black scarf tied around my neck. The black sunglasses might be overkill, though. "You never know," I say.

She stares at me, getting unnerved because she can't see my eyes. "Whatever," she finally says. "Have fun."

I grab my bag, fling open the door, and jump when I see Jake standing there, hand poised to knock.

"Hey!" I say, giving him a hug. "What are you doing here?"

"We didn't make definite plans, and I missed you. I thought I'd surprise you." He looks me over. "Going somewhere?"

"Kind of, but you should come! I'm doing market research — it's so up your alley." I fill him in on my assignment as we walk outside. "Michael, one of my bosses, gave me a packet with information. I'm supposed to start with one of the high-end stores: Bergdorf, Henri Bendel, Barneys. He also gave me a charge card with instructions to bring back at least three of my favorite designs."

I've passed the stores on Michael's list several times, but I've never gone in. Even if I had, it's not like I could have afforded to buy anything. Today will be different. If only school was this exciting!

"After you, m'lady," says Jake, holding open the door to Barneys.

I giggle. "Why, thank you, sir."

Walking into Barneys is like walking into another world. The floors look like they're made of marble, and there's a beautiful winding staircase that looks like it belongs in a mansion. And then there are the displays. Each item is hung perfectly. The shoes in the shoe department are arranged by color scheme, size, and heel height. The lighting surrounds them like a halo, showcasing each heel and strap in the best possible angle.

I think of department stores back home. There are always shoes left on the floor or shirts thrown on racks. I've even tripped over a pair of pants left in the middle of the floor.

I grab Jake's hand and we take the escalator to skirts. One item immediately catches my attention. I sketch its contrast trim and rounded hem. I expect the zipper to be in the back, but it's hidden in the front. The shirt it's paired with isn't really my style, but it's certainly unique. I sketch the silk material and tiny polka dots, then add the gold and black design on the front.

I turn to show Jake a sketch, but he's nowhere to be seen. I was so engrossed in my assignment that I didn't even notice he'd left.

"What do you think of this?" I hear him ask from a few racks down. He's holding up a dress with an argyle knit pattern.

"I like the mesh top panel and the tan and black together." I head over and check the price tag. Five hundred fifty nine dollars! For rayon and spandex?

"How much would Stefan Meyers charge for something like this?" Jake asks.

I have no idea. For all I know, Stefan's clothing might cost even more. I sketch the dress, then make a note about the price.

As we walk through the racks, my book quickly fills with sketches of jackets and dresses. I make notes about the fabrics I see and the detailed embellishments. One of my favorites is an embroidered paisley dress with a deep V-neck. I take it with me to bring back to Michael and start sketching a satin blouse with rhinestones on the collar.

"Chloe? Chloe!" Jake says, sounding irritated.

"Huh?" I say, looking up from my sketchbook. "What's wrong?" Jake looks annoyed. He must have been trying to get my attention for some time.

Jake shakes his head. "I shouldn't have just stopped by. You're obviously busy. Let's catch up later." He gives me a hug goodbye and starts to walk away.

"Wait!" I say. "This won't take all day. I'm almost done." I show him my sketches.

"They're good," he says, "but don't you want what you present to Michael to be great? You should hit one more store at least." He doesn't look annoyed anymore, just a little sad.

I start to argue. I really want to hang out with him today, but I know he's right. I need to focus. Still, is it so selfish of me to want him to tag along? "Rain check?" I ask.

"Definitely." Jake smiles, and his adorable dimple winks at me. Then he's gone.

I stand there for a moment, feeling bummed. But there's no time to waste. I have work to do. I make a beeline toward the clearance rack, paying close attention to the marked-down clothes. A cropped black sweater catches my eye, and I imagine it paired with killer black boots. The price has been marked down five times, and it's only thirty dollars! I take one for myself and grab another for Michael. Then I sketch it, adding examples in other colors.

More clearance-rack sweaters beckon. I draw a sheer silver knit with an extended front hem as well as a forest-green sweater dress with beading around the collar. Before moving to the next department, I place both outfits in my bag for Michael.

In skirts and blouses, I follow a college girl who appears to have the same taste in clothing I do. At one point, she holds up a tailored, lavender shirt with mother-of-pearl buttons down the front. She looks in the mirror and checks the price tag before slowly putting it back on the rack. When she walks away, I sketch the shirt.

Finally I tear myself away from Barneys to check out another store. More than once, I think of turning and showing Jake one of my sketches, only to realize he isn't there. I comfort myself with visions of shopping and spying and head to Bendel's.

Plunging v neck dress

Paisley Print embroidery

Black and gold

Circle Skirt w/CONTRAST TRIM

Mesh Top

Argyle Knit dress

Beaded COLLAR BLOUSE

SATIN

Bergdorf, Henri Bendel, Barneys

· Embellishments
· Pockets
· SM spring line

7

On Monday morning, Michael puts his legs up on his desk and takes a sip of coffee. "You like this knit style?" he asks, holding up my clearance sweater.

"I love it," I say.

Michael rubs his chin. "It's something to think about. I'll be passing all these drawings on to Stefan."

I wait as Michael examines the rest of my sketches. My shopping mission lasted all weekend. Sunday, I hit Bergdorf's. Whenever I caught myself missing Jake and wondering if I should have cut my shopping expedition short, I'd sketch another dress or pair of shoes. Losing myself in work is always easy.

"The spreadsheet you created of the prices makes comparing them that much easier. Seems like you had fun," Michael comments.

"Oh, my gosh — so much!" I blush, remembering my little spy getup.

"Excellent! Because I have some online detective work for you next," Michael says. "I need you to compile a list of women's fashion blogs. You're looking for the blogs with the most followers. Read the comments to gauge readers' interests. Take notes on which blogs showcase the Stefan Meyers line. It'll help us keep tabs on who to contact for more promotions."

"Got it," I reply. I head to my desk and open my laptop. But before I can do anything, my phone buzzes with a text from Jake: "Rain check? 6? Frankenstein's Tavern?"

I type back quickly. "Yes!"

With one less thing to worry about, I dive into the blogs. I check the file Michael sent me of alerts with Stefan's name and make a spreadsheet of the blogs that mention him the most. I'm working on ranking the blogs according to the number of followers, then mentions of Stefan Meyers, when Stefan himself breezes past me. "Come, Chloe!"

Me? I think. I scramble from my seat and follow Stefan to Michael's office.

"I wanted to deliver this great news in person!" Stefan announces. I see Michael trying to hide his surprise at Stefan's sudden appearance. "*Teen Design Diva* wants Chloe to be a guest judge this season!"

"Really?" I say. I can't believe it!

Michael looks less than thrilled. "When?"

"Today," Stefan says excitedly. "It's such a great opportunity. To have our intern involved in the judging keeps the spotlight on Stefan Meyers, especially with Fashion Week only two weeks away! Talk about great PR!"

"It *is* great PR," Michael admits grudgingly. "But there's still so much I'd like Chloe to do *here*."

Stefan grins at me and waves off Michael's concern. "Chloe can handle it all, can't you?"

A little voice inside me panics. *PR! Laura! Fashion Week! And now judging? Don't forget your date with Jake!* I push the panic away. "No problem," I say, giving him a confident smile.

Michael turns to me. "How's your blog report coming?" He doesn't give me a chance to answer before he turns to Stefan. "When do they need her?"

Stefan looks at his watch. "She needs to report to *Design Diva* headquarters on 45th street in an hour."

"An hour?" Michael sputters.

Stefan shrugs. "It was in a memo from two days ago, but I just saw it. Sure dodged a bullet, didn't I? We could have missed the whole thing!"

Michael grumbles something. "There's still so much to do. Finish the blog work, help with gift bags, see how we work with models, help out during the fashion show . . . the list goes on."

My mouth hangs open at all the opportunities ahead. Stefan wasn't kidding about glamour.

"The show is filming at the hotel you stayed in during the *Teen Design Diva* competition. You will be reporting to the conference room. Do you remember how to get there?"

I nod, remembering the hotel's marble floors and large conference room where we had to sew our designs. I'm excited but feel bad for leaving Michael.

"Tomorrow, it's back to the grind," I promise. "In the meantime, here's everything I've done so far." I hand him my blog spreadsheets and research.

"Have fun," Michael says reluctantly.

"Thank you!" I'm tempted to hug both him and Stefan but manage to control myself.

I leave the office with just enough time to stop in my dorm and spruce up my outfit, changing into a cute taupe dress with a black belt. If I'm going to be on TV again, I want to look my best!

The little voice in my head keeps nagging me about taking on too much, but I swat it away. Besides, Stefan made it pretty clear he wants me to go. It's not like I could have said no, even if I'd wanted to — which I didn't.

Just then, my phone buzzes with a message from Jake. "Can't wait to see you tonight!"

I think about telling him about my temporary *Design Diva* gig, but I'm sure I'll be done with the judging by then. "Me too!" I write back. Who says I can't do it all?

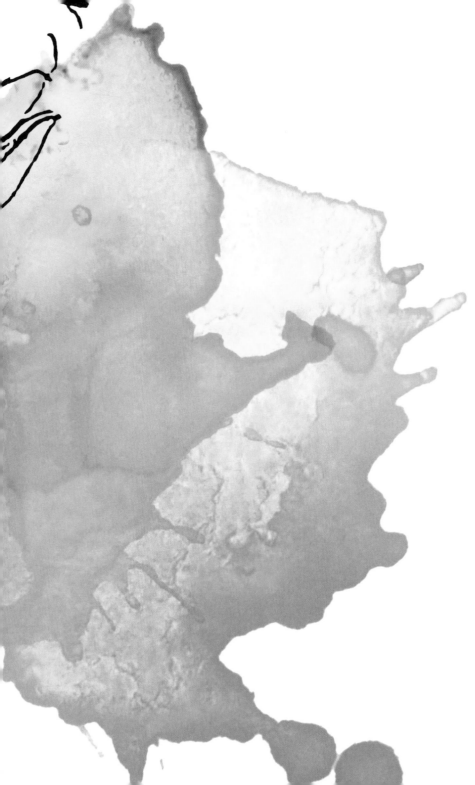

I pause at the entrance of the hotel where I completed so many challenges. *Teen Design Diva* seems ages ago. I take a deep breath and walk through the doors to the large conference room, pausing in the doorway to observe everything around me.

Contestants are sitting in groups, sometimes throwing nasty glances in their rivals' direction. The judges, Jasmine DeFabio, Hunter Bancroft, and Missy Saphire, are huddled in a corner, deep in conversation. Even though I'm not the one with designs on the line, the familiar butterflies return to my stomach.

Just then, Missy spots me. "Chloe!" she cries, running over with her arms outstretched.

Her outburst draws everyone's focus to me, and the contestants point at me and whisper to each other. They're probably wondering what the heck I'm doing here.

Missy pulls me in for a hug before dragging me toward the other judges. "Come, come."

Jasmine's warm smile catches me off guard. "Good to see you, Chloe."

"You look good," Hunter adds, his blue eyes twinkling. "Very chic."

I smooth down my ruffled dress, happy with the choice. "Thanks!"

"We're looking forward to hearing your thoughts today," says Missy. "It will be great for the contestants to get feedback from someone who's been there."

"I'm happy to help," I reply. "But . . . to be honest, I'm not sure what I'm supposed to do."

Missy smiles reassuringly. "You'll walk around with us, following our lead. You can ask questions about the designs, but don't give feedback — we don't want to clue them in to which way we're leaning. Once we start judging, feel free to express what you like and don't about the designs. Make sense?"

I nod. "I think so. But I don't want to discourage them during the judging process."

"Don't worry," says Hunter. "Everyone has his or her own style. You can be constructive without being discouraging. Maybe focus on what you like before you say how to make something better."

"That's a good idea," I say.

Jasmine glances at the clock, and her face takes on the stern look I remember. "People!" she calls to the contestants. "Please gather round. I'd like you to meet our guest judge, Miss Chloe Montgomery. I'm sure she has a few words she'd like to say."

I look nervously at Hunter, who nods encouragingly. I didn't think to have a speech prepared.

"Um," I begin. "I'm so excited to be here today. This show has provided me with an amazing opportunity, and I'm so lucky to have been a part of it." I pause and think about what helped me win. "Go with your heart. Don't worry about what someone else might say. Just design what you believe in."

The contestants clap, and I feel like a celebrity.

Missy raises her hand for silence. "Today we're going back in time to the decade of bell-bottoms, peace signs, and all things groovy," she says. "It's the 1960s, baby!"

My interest is immediately piqued. What a cool challenge to judge! There are so many possibilities. I'd take this over my first *Design Diva* challenge — animal-inspired clothing at the zoo — any day!

"Before you get carried away," Hunter says, "let me give you all the info. We're looking for pieces inspired by 1960s patterns or styles. But as with all our challenges, there's a catch. You'll need to incorporate two styles — and they must be pulled out of our hat." He reaches into a box on the judges' table and pulls out a velvet hat.

A girl with flaming red hair whose nametag reads Dani goes first. She closes her eyes, reaches into the hat, and swiftly pulls out a scrap of paper. "Op art and swirly patterns!" she calls out.

A boy with a rainbow Mohawk — Kyle, according to his nametag — is next. He takes a deep breath before slowly opening his assignment. "Tie-dye and fringe," he says. "Far out!" Everyone laughs.

A contestant with a lip ring, Carrie, walks up tentatively and draws out a slip of paper. "Peace sign and turquoise?" she says, then shuffles back to her seat. Those elements leave a lot of room for her to put her own spin on the piece. I'd have been excited, but Carrie looks confused.

The contestants continue coming up and choosing styles until all fifteen are done.

"I have some final instructions," says Jasmine. "Use this challenge as an opportunity to step out of the box. Don't make one big peace sign or flower and say that's your vision. I want to see more than that."

I stifle a giggle at Jasmine's command to think outside of the box. I heard that phrase more than once during my stint on the show. If only it offered more direction.

"You will have three hours to complete your design," says Missy. "At that point, we will discuss what you created. Then the judges will deliberate, and one of you will go home. Any questions?"

The contestants nervously look at each other. I remember that feeling. No matter how many times you go through the process, each elimination leaves you worried you'll be next.

"Ready?" says Missy. "Five, four, three, two, one — go!"

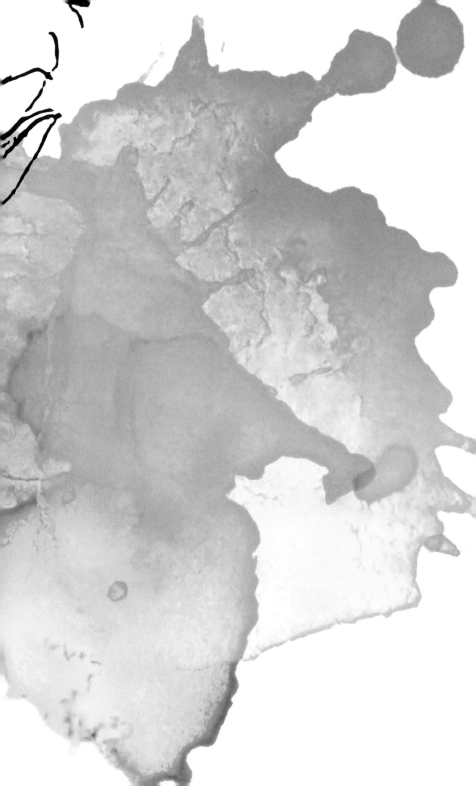

Just like when I was on the show, the contestants seem to be divided into two types of designers — those who run and grab the materials and those who take their time perfecting their vision.

I remember how crucial those beginning minutes were and give the contestants space. The camera crew, however, isn't as gracious. They surround the contestants, getting in their faces as much as possible.

"Do you miss this?" asks Jasmine.

I think about the lack of sleep and stress. "Not so much."

Jasmine laughs. "You guys were our guinea pigs. We figured out what worked and what didn't. The current contestants are benefiting from that. Sorry."

I smile. "Tell me about it. I would have killed for a challenge like this!"

"Thank you," pipes up Missy. "All my idea."

Jasmine rolls her eyes. "She's said that so many times, you'd think the *decade* was her idea."

Missy frowns at Jasmine, and the two start bickering. Just like old times. I walk away to chat with Hunter.

"How's Stefan treating you?" he asks.

"Good," I reply. "I'm learning a lot."

"That's the point. We worried a bit about whether the mentoring designers would take our winners seriously."

I think about how to respond to his unasked question. "Stefan and the designers I've worked with have been really supportive. Not everyone feels the same, but overall it's been great."

Hunter pats my shoulder. "Just brush off the rude people. That's what I do."

I nod and look at the clock. Somehow thirty minutes have already passed.

"Let's walk around," Hunter suggests.

We start at one corner, leaving the other for Missy and Jasmine. The first girl I see is wearing a nametag that reads June and is hard at work pinning a long piece of gauzy white material onto her mannequin. She pins fringe to the bottom of the gauze, and I start to envision the skirt she's designing.

On the mannequin's bust, June pins paisley material. I remember the elements she selected were gauze and paisley. I'm not sure why she decided to add fringe, but I give her the benefit of the doubt.

Hunter is about to speak to her when the camera crew suddenly pounces. "Let's get back to her," he says.

The next contestant, Dani, is working barefoot. Her flaming red hair is now tied back with a scrap of fabric.

"Want to tell us about your design?" Hunter asks as we approach.

"Love to!" says Dani. She talks enthusiastically about her black-and-white op-art tank dress, focusing on the swirly pattern she's adding. All the while, she continues working, not taking her eyes off her piece. "I'm going to add sleeves, but I have to figure out what will work. Of course, the sleeves might throw everything out of whack, but what can you do? I'm a fly-by-the-seat-of-your-pants kind of girl."

"I wish I could be more like that," I say. "Good luck."

Our next stop is Kyle, the boy with the rainbow Mohawk. He's frantically pinning and cutting something resembling a micro-mini. Suddenly he starts pacing and muttering about thread and adhesive tape. His sneaker catches on the carpet, and he crashes into his mannequin. It tumbles on top of him, and the cameras are immediately in his face, capturing each gruesome second.

Hunter stops to talk to him, but I give him space. I see Missy has moved on to Carrie, and go join her.

"What do you think so far?" asks Missy.

"I feel for all of them," I say.

"You can be the softie today," Missy says with a smile. "Speaking of, should we discuss Carrie's, um, creation?"

Missy steps aside, and I see all of Carrie's design. Unfortunately, she didn't stop at the two patterns she picked. The hemp culottes she's working on could have been paired with a turquoise belt or a beaded peace sign. Instead, she's laying it on thick with flower power. The hems are embroidered with flowers, as are the knees and belt. The turquoise peasant blouse has peace signs bordering the sleeves. To tie it all together, Carrie added beading and fringe.

I rack my brain for words of encouragement. "You really went all out," I manage. "What made you go beyond the two patterns you originally chose?"

"The more patterns, the better," Carrie replies, beaming. "I'm also adding beads to the ends of the fringe. Can't hurt, right?"

It's already a disaster. More beading won't matter. I wish I could tell her to start over and stick with just turquoise and peace signs, but guidance isn't allowed. "Do what you think is best," I say, smiling.

"Chloe's too nice," Missy tells Jasmine when we're standing beside her a few minutes later.

Jasmine looks at Carrie's design. "Don't tell me she was optimistic about that monstrosity . . ."

I shift uncomfortably. Carrie's piece *is* a mess, but it's unfair to let one bad decision determine everything. "Everyone has a bad day," I mumble.

"Well, she's had a few," says Jasmine. She looks at the clock — one hour left. Two hours until I see Jake. Taping is sure to be done by then.

"She has promise," Hunter says, joining us. "But not everyone is cut out for these competitions. It's a lot of pressure."

The judges continue examining the designs, and I try to catch up with those I've missed. One piece immediately catches my attention. The designer, Jared, has his long, dark hair pulled back into a ponytail. His mannequin is dressed in a free-flowing, white cotton skirt and a belt embellished with turquoise stones and beads. The top is a nod to the form-fitting clothes of the sixties.

"I like how you incorporated the turquoise as well as the form-fitting element," I tell him.

"I was trying to meld the two styles of the time," says Jared. "There was the group with the tighter, shorter clothing, and then there was the hippie movement. The

BLACK & WHITE COLOR PALETTE

OP-ART SWIRLS

SLEEVELESS MINIDRESS

DANI'S BLACK & WHITE TANK DRESS

teen **DESIGN DIVA**

JARED'S
HIPPIE & MOD
STYLES BLENDED

BEADED
NECKLINE

PEASANT
SHIRT

BELT OF
TURQUOISE
BEADS &
GEMSTONES

WHITE
LONG-SLEEVE
DRESS

FRINGE

CARRIE'S
PEACE SIGNS, TURQUOISE
BLOUSE & CULOTTES

turquoise stones and beading are a nod to my Native American heritage. The culture really influenced fashion in the sixties."

"I'm looking forward to seeing the completed design," I say, moving on. Jared's design is my favorite so far, and his connection to his heritage reminds me of my connection to my grandfather's cowboy style. Gramps was well known in the rodeo world, and his death — months before the *Design Diva* audition — was really hard for me. But thinking of all he accomplished and letting his memory be the inspiration for my designs helped me stand out.

"Thirty minutes!" calls Hunter.

Contestants immediately start scrambling, flinging their materials in all directions. This is the part the cameras love, but I move to a corner and watch everything unfold from there. I focus on a girl with spiky hair who's frantically putting the finishing touches on a fringed vest. If only she'd left it at that. Instead, she's paired the vest with a dress covered in peace signs and flowers.

"Good thing we're letting two go today," says Jasmine as the judges huddle beside me.

"What?" I say, surprised. "I thought you told the contestants one would be eliminated."

"We did," says Missy. "But that's today's twist. Sometimes you have to mix it up. We didn't mean to leave you in the dark."

I think about the twists during my *Design Diva* competition — everything from endless hand sewing to two tasks in one day. I hated being blind-sided. And it doesn't feel any better as a judge than it did as a contestant.

"Time!" yells Hunter. Fifteen pairs of eyes stare at us, dying to know their fate.

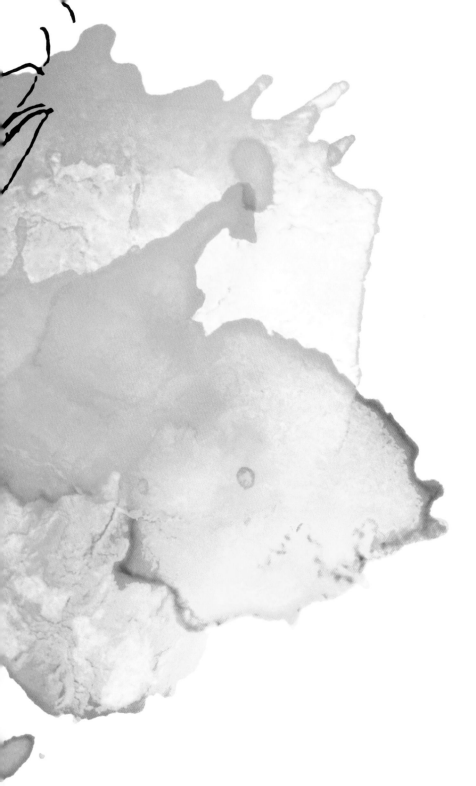

I follow Jasmine, Hunter, and Missy to the judges' table and wait for them to take the lead.

"We are so pleased to see such a diverse collection today," Hunter begins. "Your individuality really shone through in the challenge."

I nod but then remember that eliminations always start off positive. Then, a judge brings the mood down.

"Unfortunately," Jasmine says, fulfilling my prophecy, "some of you got buried in your unique vision and lost sight of what's fashionable. More is not always better, people."

I see several faces fall and want to say something encouraging, but it's not my turn. Instead, I stay quiet as the judges go from one contestant to the other, giving feedback that's often biting. I do my best to add something supportive.

"Matthew, tell us about your piece, please," Hunter says, calling forward a boy whose design I didn't get a chance to inspect. Seeing it now is a shock. Multiple colors and psychedelic images take over the design. He also added fringe, beading, and stones.

"Sure!" says Matthew. "I wanted a bold design and added several styles and patterns to achieve that. The minidress is modeled after Jackie O's trademark dresses —"

"Sorry, no," Jasmine interrupts. "Mrs. Onassis would have never worn that."

I cringe. Was Jasmine always this mean?

To his credit, Matthew remains unflustered. "Perhaps that's only because such an item wasn't available." He winks, and Jasmine snorts. "Anyway, I wanted to combine Mrs. O's style with the hippie movement."

Missy shifts uncomfortably in her chair. "I'll defer to Chloe on this one."

I swallow. "Hi, Matthew. Well, um, I think you're very brave. You had an idea in your head, and you definitely went with it. Kudos for sticking to your guns," I say diplomatically. I'm not going to crush his dreams.

Matthew falls back into line, and Hunter grins. "Nice work, Chloe," he whispers.

"Thanks," I say, hoping the next contestant is easier.

"Dani, come on down!" Hunter says. As she gets closer, he adds, "The great thing about Dani is that she never fails to surprise us."

Dani smiles. "I do my best."

I look at her finished product, complete with sheer black-and-white sleeves.

"I worried the sleeves might be overkill," Dani says, "but I like how they came out."

"Overkill is definitely not a word that comes to mind here," Missy says. "As usual, you've managed to combine a variety of ideas to create something different. I'm glad you took the risk."

"I agree," I chime in. "The black-and-white pattern is hypnotizing."

"Well done, Dani," says Hunter. "June, you're up next."

I sit up straighter. When I left June, she still had two patterns to complete.

"I've always loved the flowing skirts of the sixties," June begins. "But I wanted to take it a step further, so I added fringe to the hem. It complements the paisley bodice. I also added some light beading to the V-neck."

"Hmm," says Jasmine. "I like the color and the beading, but the fringe doesn't work for me."

JUNE'S
GAUZE & PAISLEY
SKIRT & SHIRT

PAISLEY
BODICE

GAUZE
SKIRT

Paisley
Top

Gauze
Skirt

Fringed
hem

FRINGE HEM

teen
DESIGN
DIVA

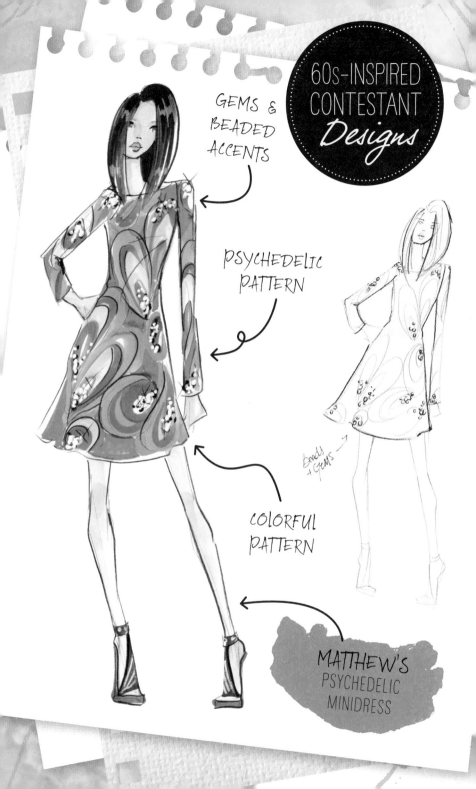

GEMS & BEADED ACCENTS

60s-INSPIRED CONTESTANT *Designs*

PSYCHEDELIC PATTERN

Beads + Gems

COLORFUL PATTERN

MATTHEW'S PSYCHEDELIC MINIDRESS

"I agree," says Hunter. "You have something really good here, but the fringe takes away from the design."

June's eyes beg me to say something different, but the truth is, I hate the fringe too. "This design is so promising," I start. "Your choice of green works well with the skirt, and I love the beading."

"Thank you," June says.

The judges continue with the other contestants. Kyle's design survived his fall, but it's still a mess. His bell-bottom pants have bells at the hems, and the shirt is a combination of polka dots and wavy lines. Pulling it all together is a tie-dyed macramé vest.

When it's my turn, I stick to keeping things positive. "It's a little busy for me, but I admire your ambition," I say.

Jasmine snorts. "Last but not least," she says, "we have Jared."

"Like some of my previous designs, I wanted to include my Native American background," Jared says, stepping forward. "My grandfather, who recently passed, was always such a force in my life. He was so proud of our heritage."

Jared chokes up, and a lump forms in my throat too. Just like me, he has a connection to his grandfather. And just like me, he's used it for inspiration.

"Your inspiration clearly shines through," Jasmine says, her voice surprisingly kind. "You've merged two elements of sixties style very successfully."

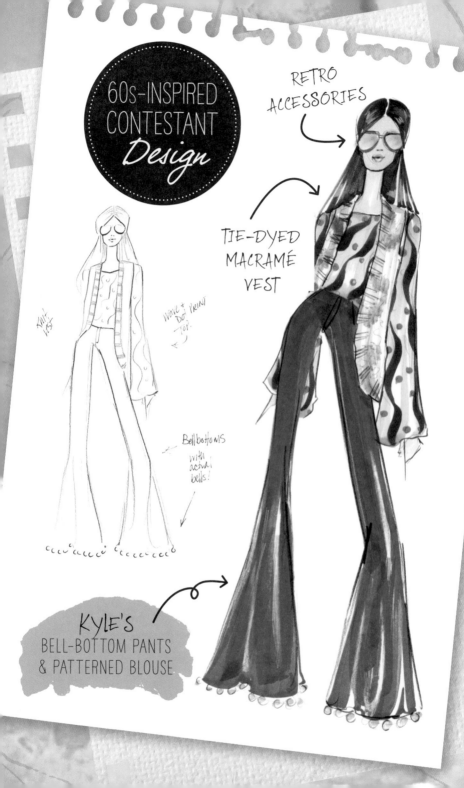

60s-INSPIRED CONTESTANT *Design*

RETRO ACCESSORIES

TIE-DYED MACRAMÉ VEST

Wave & print dot print top.

Bell bottoms with actual bells!

KYLE'S
BELL-BOTTOM PANTS
& PATTERNED BLOUSE

"I like the addition of the turquoise stones around the collar. The stones and belt really pull the pieces together," I add.

"Thank you," says Jared, his voice stronger.

"Thank you for all your hard work and creativity," Hunter says. "Now it's time for the judges to deliberate. We'll call you back in when we have a decision."

The contestants leave the room, and Hunter, Missy, Jasmine, and I begin debating the positives and negatives of each design. I glance at the clock. Jake and I are supposed to meet in an hour.

"Wasn't Jared's design the best?" I ask.

"His was fantastic, but there are positives in many of the contestants' designs," Missy tells me. "Besides, we have to let two go, and there were too many problematic designs to make that decision easy."

"I liked Dani's design too," I offer.

"Agreed," Hunter says.

We continue to deliberate and have no trouble placing Dani and Jared into the favorites category. Choosing the bottom designers is tougher.

Without the contestants present, I can speak more freely. "June's fringe was overkill," I say. "But it was just one extra addition. Carrie's and Matthew's designs had more issues. They should have stuck to two styles each."

Jasmine nods appreciatively. "I would have liked to have seen more of this Chloe with the contestants," she says.

I shake my head. "You guys are great, but they expect negative feedback from you. I'd rather be positive. They all tried their best."

Hunter winks at me. "I'm with Chloe. No need to make her into the big, bad meanie."

"What about Kyle?" Missy asks.

"His design had too much happening. But at least it seemed more cohesive than Carrie's and Matthew's," I say.

"I agree," Missy says. "It was better — but barely."

"So we're set?" I say. I look at the clock, feeling anxious. I don't want to flake out on Jake.

"I think so," Hunter says, "but let's recap."

I try to stay focused as they review the positives and negatives of each design. After a half hour, I look at the clock again. I'm supposed to meet Jake in twenty minutes. There's no way I'll make it. I tap my toes.

"You have somewhere to be, Chloe?" asks Jasmine. Her voice is cool. "If you need to leave, go. We'll explain it to the producers — somehow."

"It's okay," I say. "I just need to tell someone I'll be late."

I take out my phone to text Jake, but the battery has died. Could this get any worse? Jasmine is still staring at me. I sigh and put on my best happy face. "I'm all yours."

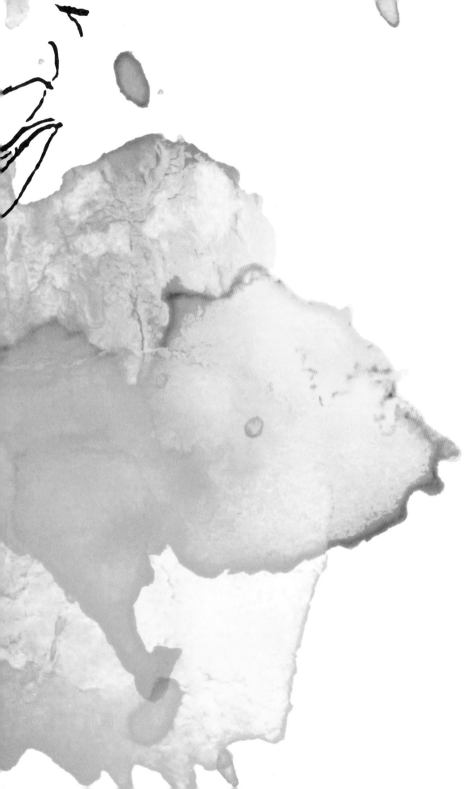

11

The *Design Diva* deliberations seem to go on forever. By the time the judges announce (unsurprisingly) that Jared is the winner and Carrie and Matthew are eliminated, I've given up all hope of seeing Jake.

Just as I grab my bag to go back to my dorm, Missy says, "Before all our designers leave for the night, I'm sure Chloe wouldn't mind answering any questions you might have."

I put my bag back on my seat and slap on my most encouraging smile. "Of course not." At this point, there's no meeting with Jake, anyway.

Hunter, Missy, and Jasmine gather the contestants and arrange chairs in a circle. Dani raises her hand first. "Which of the designs you did on the show was your favorite?" she asks.

"Definitely the one for the Toys 'R' Us challenge. I was feeling down and not sure how to make something out-of-the box." The contestants laugh at this and nod, relating to it. "But then I thought about how to make the piece my own. The local fair back in my hometown was a big inspiration for me when I designed my cotton candy-inspired skirt for that challenge."

"How did you sew without machines?" asks June.

"Very stressfully," I say, and everyone laughs again.

"Tell us about your internship," Kyle says.

"It's been amazing," I say. "Stefan Meyers lets me be very hands-on. If you guys think the competition is getting too hard, just think of the internship. It's worth it."

"Are there any mean girls?" asks June. "Like Nina LeFleur from your season?"

I think of Madison and frame my answer carefully. "There will always be people who try to get the best of you. The key is to keep believing in yourself."

I know my answer sounded too perfect, but it's true. Besides, the cameras are still rolling. I don't want my words to be edited into something vicious.

"What do you like best about your internship?" asks Jared.

"Learning new things," I say. "Going into this competition, I thought I had a good handle on fashion design. Even more so after winning. But working for Stefan Meyers has made me realize that there's so much more to learn. I want my own label one day, and there's a lot to know about running it."

I'm starting to feel more at ease and less anxious when someone calls out, "Whatever happened with you and that cute boy?"

I blush. Jake gave me a big hug onstage after I won, and the cameras panned to him during the last challenge, so it's not surprising the contestants remember him. "Um, we're still friends," I say. *Hopefully*, I want to add. I imagine Jake waiting for me, trying to call me, and then walking back to his apartment — alone. It makes me sad.

I steer the conversation elsewhere. "What do you wish would be different about the competition?" I ask. I wish someone had asked this during my season.

"More sleep would be nice," says Jared.

"A little more time to start our designs before everyone swarms in," says Kyle.

I nod. I can appreciate that. I spend a few more minutes chatting before wrapping things up. I give the new crop of designers my e-mail in case they have more questions.

"Stay in touch," Jasmine tells me. "We're rooting for you out there."

I hug the judges goodbye and walk back to my dorm. It was a great day, but I wonder if I could have done things differently. Should I have left? What would have happened if I had? I unlock the door to my suite, wanting to charge my phone and be alone, but Bailey is sitting in the common room.

"Hey," I say as I plug in my phone.

She puts down her sketch. "What's wrong? You look like you're going to cry. Oh! Before I forget, Jake was here looking for you. Did he find you?"

I look at her miserably and tell her the whole story.

"Ugh. That stinks," Bailey says when I finish.

"I know. And I feel so ungrateful. I got to be a *Design Diva* judge, which was amazing, but I really wanted to see Jake." I shake my head. "I should have left."

Bailey stares at me like I've lost my mind. "Are you insane? You did *not* just say that, Chloe. This is your dream we're talking about! I know you're still in high school, but fashion design is all about opportunities and catching a break. Talent too, but there are a lot of talented designers out there. You don't just throw away an opportunity like that!"

I've never seen Bailey annoyed at me, but she clearly is now. "Sorry," I mumble.

Bailey sighs. "I don't mean to lecture you, but so many people would kill for what you have. I mean, if someone told you last year to walk a mile in a pair of Manolo Blahniks for this chance, wouldn't you have done it?"

I nod. Miles. Marathons. Anything. My phone buzzes, signaling that it finally has some juice, and I see six texts from Jake, all asking where I am. The last one says, "Guess you're busy. Hope you're okay."

I immediately call Jake's cell, but it goes straight to voicemail. I leave a message saying how sorry I am and explaining what happened.

When I put the phone down, Bailey does the same with her sketchpad. "If it's meant to be, he'll understand. Get some sleep. You'll feel better in the morning."

I swallow, feeling a pit in my stomach. "Thanks for listening."

"Any time."

I start to go into my room when Bailey says, "Chloe?"

I turn around.

"You're really talented. Don't let anything stand in your way."

I nod. "Thanks again."

I get ready for bed and try to focus on all the positives ahead of me. All the things I've always wanted. Based on what Michael said, I've barely experienced PR. That's to happen in the days to come. I close my eyes and imagine Fashion Week, runways, models, and my designs. I imagine Stefan saying how lucky he is to have such a fabulous intern. I keep these images in my head and don't let them get away.

Author Bio

MARGIE

Margaret Gurevich has wanted to be a writer since second grade and has written for many magazines, including *Girls' Life*, *SELF*, and *Ladies' Home Journal*. Her first young adult novel, *Inconvenient*, was a Sydney Taylor Notable Book for Teens, and her second novel, *Pieces of Us*, garnered positive reviews from *Kirkus*, *VOYA*, and *Publishers Weekly*, which called it "painfully believable." When not writing, Margaret enjoys hiking, cooking, reading, watching too much television, and spending time with her husband and son.

Illustrator Bio

BROOKE

Brooke Hagel is a fashion illustrator based in New York City. While studying fashion design at the Fashion Institute of Technology, she began her career as an intern, working in the wardrobe department of *Sex and the City*, the design studios of Cynthia Rowley, and the production offices of *Saturday Night Live*. After graduating, Brooke began designing and styling for Hearst Magazines, contributing to *Harper's Bazaar*, *House Beautiful*, *Seventeen*, and *Esquire*. Brooke is now a successful illustrator with clients including *Vogue*, *Teen Vogue*, *InStyle*, Dior, Brian Atwood, Hugo Boss, Barbie, Gap, and Neutrogena.